The Curse of the Jungle Treasure

Yanitzia Canetti and Debra Hess

SCHOLASTIC INC.

New York   Toronto   London   Auckland   Sydney
Mexico City   New Delhi   Hong Kong   Buenos Aires

Illustrations
Monica Melnychuck

Text copyright © 2003 by Scholastic Inc.
Illustrations copyright © 2003 by Monica Melnychuck.
All rights reserved. Published by Scholastic Inc.
Printed in the U.S.A.

ISBN 0-439-59776-5

SCHOLASTIC, SCHOLASTIC ACTION, and associated logos and designs are trademarks and/or registered trademarks of Scholastic Inc.

LEXILE is a registered trademark of MetaMetrics, Inc.

2 3 4 5 6 7 8 9 10   23   12 11 10 09 08 07 06 05 04 03

Contents

Welcome to This Book

If you knew about a treasure hidden deep in a jungle, would you look for it? Would you go if you knew that the treasure was cursed?

The three kids in this story decided to go for the gold. It all starts when Tony's mom makes him spend the summer with his cousins in Peru. He thinks it's going to be boring. But his cousins have an exciting treasure hunt planned.

It turns out to be an adventure of a lifetime. Will they be rich? Will they survive?

Target Words

These words will help you solve the curse of the jungle treasure.

- **attitude:** opinions and feelings about someone or something

  Tony has a real problem with his attitude.

- **legend:** a story handed down from earlier times

  The curse of Chavin was part of a legend.

- **terrified:** to be greatly frightened

  Tony did not want to admit that he was terrified in the jungle.

Reader Tips

Here's how to get the most out of this book.

- **Illustrations** Illustrations provide details about the characters that aren't in the story. Look at the illustration on page 12. What details do you notice that are not in the story?

- **Summarize** A summary is a short report about the most important events of a story. As you read, summarize the most important events. That way you will be sure to follow the plot and better understand what you've read.

1

The Worst Summer Ever

Will Tony's mother really make him stay in South America all summer?

South America was his mother's idea. Tony wanted to go to sleep-away camp with his friends. It was going to be the best summer ever at Camp Seneca. Tony was fourteen years old. He was going to learn to be a **counselor.** That meant he would get to boss around the little kids all summer. But Mama said he had to go to Peru. She said Uncle Marco needed help fixing up his new house. She said a summer in South America with his cousins would be fun. Tony didn't think it sounded like fun at all.

The plane ride from Florida to Peru had been okay. And Tony had to admit that his cousins, Mateo and Julia, seemed nice enough.

Julia was the same age as Tony. She had long dark hair and sparkly eyes. Tony knew that his friends in Miami would like her a lot. Mateo was ten. Maybe Tony could boss him around. Still, the car trip from the airport to the house had taken all day. Tony was pretty sure they were in the middle of nowhere. He was also pretty sure that there would be no skate parks, swimming pools, or game cubes here. It was going to be a long, boring summer.

He called his mother. "I can't believe you're making me stay here," he **grumbled.** "It's a thousand degrees. And I've never seen so many bugs in my entire life."

"Well, of course there are bugs. You're in the middle of the jungle," said his mother.

"Why would anyone live here?" said Tony.

"Give it a chance, honey. You've only been there one day."

"It's enough. Please let me come home and go to camp."

He could hear his mother sigh all the way in Florida.

"There are a lot of bugs here, too, Tony."

"Please, Mom."

"Put Marco on the phone," she said.

Tony got his uncle and handed him the phone. Uncle Marco was okay, he guessed. It must be hard raising two kids on your own. And now he had an extra kid for the whole summer. What were they going to do while Uncle Marco was at work all day?

Tony wandered into the kitchen. Julia and Mateo were sitting at the table. They were eating something Tony had never seen before.

"Hey Antonio," said Mateo as Tony entered the kitchen.

"I told you it's Tony."

"You want something to eat?" asked Julia.

"Sure. You got anything normal?" Tony asked. He knew he was being mean, but he didn't seem to be able to stop himself.

"Sure," said Julia, smiling. "We've got fried lizard on a roll."

Mateo laughed at his sister's joke.

"That's supposed to be funny? Well, it's not." grumbled Tony.

"It *is* funny!" said Mateo, still laughing. "Julia, you crack me up."

"Look," said Tony. "I don't want to spend the summer here. And I'm sure that you don't want me to either. So let's just stay out of each other's way, okay?"

Tony definitely had a bad **attitude.** He gave his cousins his meanest look and left the room. He made sure to slam the door on his way out.

Heads Up!

Look up attitude *in the glossary. Why do you think Tony has such a bad attitude?*

2

Jungle Adventure

Tony isn't scared of anything. Or is he?

Tony was called to dinner at five. He thought it was kind of early, but he was starving.

"What is this?" he asked, pushing the food around his plate with a fork.

"It's great!" said Mateo, with a mouthful of food.

"Just try it," said Uncle Marco.

"Not until you tell me what it is," said Tony.

"It's *Papa Rellena*," said Julia. "Now eat it."

Tony studied the food on his plate. He took a breath, cut into the food, and popped a piece in his mouth.

"It's delicious!" he said, surprised. "Now tell me what it is."

"It's potatoes stuffed with meat," said Mateo.

"So," said Uncle Marco, "I have to work tomorrow. But I thought on Saturday we could take a ride on the jungle boat."

Tony rolled his eyes.

"Is there a problem, Antonio?"

"I told you—it's Tony."

"Is there a problem, Tony?"

Tony shrugged. "What is it—a kiddie ride?"

Uncle Marco smiled. "It's a boat ride through the jungle."

"Yeah!" shouted Mateo. "And it's really scary. There are alligators and everything."

"I'm not scared of anything," said Tony.

Uncle Marco sighed and stood up to clear his plate from the table.

"What am I going to do with this guy?" he muttered under his breath.

But no one was listening. Mateo was busy whispering something to Julia. Tony was trying to hear what Mateo was saying.

―Heads Up!―

Look at the illustration on the next page. What do you notice about Tony and Julia?

Uncle Marco is at the sink. Mateo is whispering to Julia. Tony is trying to hear what Mateo is saying.

3

The Statue of Chavin

Will the kids go on a treasure hunt—
for a real treasure?

Uncle Marco had already left for work when Tony woke up the next morning. As he was **shuffling** down the hallway to the kitchen, he heard Julia's voice.

"I'm telling you it's too dangerous," said Julia.

"Oh, come on, Julia," Mateo **pleaded.** It would be sooo cool. Even Tony would think it was scary."

"I don't care what Tony would think," said Julia. "It's too dangerous. You know no one has ever gotten out alive."

"We could," said Mateo. "I have it all worked out."

"No," said Julia. "And that's final. Not a word of it to Tony, okay?"

"Not a word of *what* to Tony?" said Tony, walking into the room.

Julia **glared** at Mateo.

"Nothing," she said brightly. "Are you hungry? Do you want breakfast?"

"I want to know what you're talking about," Tony said.

"It's the curse of Chavin," Mateo blurted out.

"Mateo! You promised," said Julia.

"No, I didn't," said Mateo.

"No, he didn't," said Tony.

"'I give up," said Julia.

Over a breakfast of *huevos rancheros,* Julia and Mateo told Tony about the curse of Chavin.

"It's a **legend,** really," said Julia.

"What she means is that no one knows if it's really true," said Mateo.

"What's Chavin?" asked Tony.

Heads Up!

Do you think that Tony is starting to get interested? Why or why not?

"Chavin is a statue," said Julia.

Tony laughed. "A statue, big deal."

"See, Mateo? He's not interested. And it's too hot anyway. Let's go to the waterfall. Don't forget to clear your plates when you're done eating."

Julia left the room.

"It's in the middle of the jungle," said Mateo.

"What is?"

"The statue. It's in the middle of the jungle and it's surrounded by all kinds of weird things that protect it, like snakes and fire pits. No one who has ever tried to touch it has lived. It's cursed."

"Well, why would anyone want to touch it?" asked Tony. He was pretending not to be interested, but Mateo could tell he wanted to know.

"Because of the gold," said Mateo. "There's like—I don't know—a million dollars of gold in there."

"Inside the statue?" asked Tony.

"I think so." said Julia, walking back into the room. "I can't really say for sure. No one really knows."

"Yeah, because they're all dead. That's the curse!" yelled Mateo.

"I don't believe in curses. So let's go get it!" said Tony. "Do you know where it is?"

"Mateo says he does," said Julia. "He's been bugging me to take him there for months."

"I learned about it in school," said Mateo proudly. "Chavin is this really, really old, uh—" Mateo scratched his head as he searched his memory for the right word.

"**Culture,**" said Julia.

"Yeah. Culture," said Mateo. "And there is a statue left over. It's been there for billions of years."

"Thousands," Julia corrected him.

Mateo rolled his eyes.

"How would we get there?" asked Tony.

"Yeah, Mateo. How would we get there?" asked Julia.

"Raver can take us," said Mateo.

"That's a pretty good idea," said Julia.

"Who's Raver?" asked Tony.

"My best friend's brother," said Julia. "He's one of the tour guides. I guess we could get a ride there with him today."

"We can tell him that we're going to show Tony the wildlife **preserve,**" said Mateo.

Julia had to admit that her little brother really did have it all worked out.

Heads Up!

Would you go looking for a treasure that was cursed?

It's Alive!

Are there really killer birds in the jungle?

No one said a word for the entire car ride to the jungle entrance.

Mateo had a hand-drawn map **clutched** in one hand and a list of things to be careful of in the other. Julia carried a knapsack of water, snacks, and flashlights. She hadn't told the others, but she brought a camera, too.

Raver dropped them off at the entrance to the wildlife preserve and told them if they wanted a lift back home they should be there at four. As soon as he left, Tony looked at Mateo.

Now which way?

Mateo looked at his map. Then he pointed in the direction of a dark path, overgrown with leaves.

"This way!" he said.

They walked for almost an hour. At first, Tony thought it was exciting. He had never been in a jungle before and he could picture himself grabbing onto a vine and swinging from tree to tree, yelling like Tarzan. Of course, Julia wouldn't let him do it. She said the vines weren't really strong enough and he would get hurt. She was starting to bug him. The heat was also starting to bug him. And the bugs were really bugging him!

Suddenly, Tony heard a strange noise.

"Sssh—listen," he whispered to his cousins. "What's that sound?"

"It sounds like wings flapping," said Mateo.

"Giant wings," said Julia.

"No, I'm serious," said Tony.

"So are we," said Julia.

"It's the bird that guards the entrance to the cave," Mateo whispered loudly.

Heads Up!

Summarize what has happened in the story so far. Can you guess what will happen next?

"What cave?" asked Tony.

"The cave where the statue is."

There was no mistaking the sound now. It was the flapping of wings. And it was coming from behind a huge tree right in front of them.

"It's just a bird," said Tony. "Big deal."

"It's just a *killer* bird," said Mateo.

At that moment, there was a shower of leaves and the tops of the trees all began moving.

Julia screamed and started running.

"Wait!" cried Mateo. "Look!"

In the sky above them, hundreds of colorful birds flew in a group.

"Oh, my mistake, it wasn't the killer bird after all," said Mateo, laughing.

Julia grinned at Tony. "Good thing you don't get scared," she said.

Tony rolled his eyes. Next time, he would be ready for their little jokes.

They walked deeper into the jungle. Every now and then a snake would slither past or a strange sound would fill the air.

None of it bothered Tony until the smell.

It was horrible. It hung in the air and filled their mouths and noses. Tony thought he was going to be sick. He leaned against a tree and covered his mouth. Then, something in front of him moved.

Tony screamed and jumped back. The something was huge and hairy and purple. Spikes poked out of its slime-green paws. The smell was coming from the spikes. What was it? Tony gulped and pointed. He couldn't speak. The thing moved again. It was alive!

"What is it?" Tony whispered. He did not want the thing to hear them.

Mateo grabbed a stick and moved forward. He was going to poke it.

"No!" cried Tony. "Don't make it mad."

Mateo poked at it anyway.

The creature opened its mouth and chomped down on the stick.

Tony jumped back.

"Don't worry," Mateo said. "It's just a flesh-eating plant. I've seen one like it before."

"That could have been you, Tony," Julia said.

"Or at least your finger." She laughed.

Tony didn't think it was funny. The jungle was starting to give him the creeps.

> **─Heads Up!─**
>
> *Do you think Tony is scared? Do you think he was telling the truth when he said nothing scared him?*

5

Mateo is Missing!

Mateo is gone and the treasure is nowhere to be seen.

It seemed to Tony as if the smell kept following them. But after a while it went away.

Tony took his hand away from his nose.

"Are we almost there?" he called over his shoulder to Mateo.

But there was no answer. Tony turned around. Mateo was not behind him.

"Hey Julia," he called up ahead. "Is Mateo with you?"

"What do you mean? Where is he?" said Julia. Tony could hear the **panic** in her voice.

"I don't know," Tony said. "He was here just a minute ago."

"I'm down here!" Mateo shouted.

Mateo's voice is coming from a hole in the ground.

Mateo's voice sounded like it was coming from a hole in the ground.

Julia bent down and called into the hole.

"Are you okay?"

"Yes. I just—I can't get out," said Mateo. "And it's dark in here. And . . ." Mateo screamed.

"Mateo!" Julia called.

But there was no answer.

Julia started clawing at the hole.

"Julia—wait," said Tony. "You'll never get to him that way."

"Well, what do you think we should do?" said Julia, sitting back on her heels. There were tears streaming down her face. She wiped at them with a dirty hand.

Tony felt the ground. It was wet. He could hear running water in the distance.

"Come on," he said. He held his hand out to Julia. She took it and Tony helped her up.

"Do you see the way the ground is wet here and you can hear water in the distance?" he asked.

"So?" said Julia.

"And did you hear the way Mateo's voice was echoing when he called to us?"

"So?" Julia repeated.

"So I think he's in a cave and the opening is over that hill," said Tony.

"Oh yeah?" Julia sniffled. "Since when are you an expert?"

He shrugged. "We studied caves in school."

Julia smiled. "Well," she said. "There's a river over there."

"Let's go!" said Tony.

They ran over the hill towards the river. Tony hoped he was right about the cave. He hoped they could save Mateo. As he ran after Julia, he couldn't help thinking about the curse. Maybe it was real, after all.

Heads Up!

Do you think Tony has changed since the beginning of the book? If so, how?

6

There's No Such Thing As Vampires

Vampires aren't real. Or are they?

Julia was a fast runner and she reached the river first. Tony heard her screams before he got to her. She was standing at the bank of the river, staring at some white things sticking up.

"Bones!" Julia gasped. She grabbed Tony's arm. "I bet these are the bones of the last guy who went searching for Chavin."

A shiver ran up and down Tony's back as he bent down and looked at the bones.

"I think these are rocks," he said.

"HELP!" a voice echoed.

"Mateo!" yelled Julia. She ran in the direction of the voice. "Mateo—are you all right?"

"I'm stuck!" called Mateo.

"Keep yelling so we can follow your voice!" Tony called to Mateo. "He must be around here someplace," Tony said to Julia.

They followed the sound of Mateo's voice to an opening in the hill and crawled in after the small boy. They found themselves in a dark cave. They turned on their flashlights and found Mateo right away. He was okay, but his foot was trapped under a log. Tony and Julia lifted it up and Mateo slid out from beneath the log.

"Let's get out of here," said Mateo. "This place is creepy."

Tony flashed his light onto the top of the cave. Hundreds of eyes stared back at him.

"What the?…" Tony stumbled backwards.

"Run!" yelled Mateo.

"Calm down you two," said Julia. "Those are just **vampire bats.**"

"Vampires! Will they suck our blood?" asked Tony.

"No, silly. You're not their type," Julia said. "Blood type, that is."

"But don't they like any kind of blood?" asked Tony. He knew they did. Well, he was pretty sure they did. Well, he thought he read somewhere that they did. Anyway, he didn't want to wait to find out. He liked his blood where it was—in his body.

"On second thought, I think they like the blood of people from Florida," said Julia.

"Very funny," said Tony.

Julia and Mateo burst out laughing. Tony tried to look angry. But he had to grin.

Just then, a cloud of bats began to fly in circles. The beating of their wings made a ton of noise.

"Now, let's get out of here!" yelled Julia. The three kids raced out of the cave.

Heads Up!

Do you think Mateo, Julia, and Tony are going to find the treasure? Why or why not?

7

Treasure!

If they do find the treasure, what else will they find?

The screaming was next. Horrible, high-pitched screaming. Tony covered his ears.

"The monkeys," said Mateo.

"Yeah, I see the monkeys," said Tony. "But where are those screams coming from?" He felt like he might scream, too.

"They're called howler monkeys. They like to scream. They aren't dangerous," said Mateo. "Are you scared?"

"No. Of course not," said Tony. But he *was* scared. He was in the middle of a jungle. There were flesh-eating plants and vampire bats and screaming monkeys. And he and his cousins were after a treasure that was cursed.

Mateo had stopped walking. He was standing at the beginning of a stone path.

"I think Chavin's cave is up ahead," he said. He broke into a run, sped under a **canopy** of leaves, and disappeared.

Suddenly, Tony and Julia heard him scream.

They found Mateo crouched behind a tree, pointing at a statue at the entrance to a cave. It was a stone monster, part human and part jaguar, with huge fangs dangling from its mouth. Snakes wound themselves in and out of its empty eye sockets.

"Chavin," gasped Julia.

Tony's legs shook as he moved closer to the statue.

"What are you doing?" yelled Mateo from where he hid behind the tree.

"I thought you said there was gold inside," said Tony, his eyes on the snakes.

"*Maybe* there's gold inside," said Julia.

Tony moved closer and closer until he was standing just inches away from the statue.

"Don't do it, Tony!" screamed Mateo.

"It's not worth it!" Julia cried.

But Tony hadn't come this far to go home with no gold. Slowly, he reached toward the open mouth of the statue. He could feel the beads of sweat dripping down his neck and arms.

He waited for a snake to slither out of the mouth and down the statue. Then he plunged his hand into the mouth of the monster. He felt something, grabbed onto it, and pulled. A mud-covered sack came out in his hand. He sprang away just as another snake slithered out.

"Let's go!" he yelled. He took off back in the direction they had come from. He could hear Mateo and Julia behind him.

They ran until they were out of breath, and then collapsed in a clearing. Julia and Mateo watched as Tony opened the sack. He peeked in and his mouth fell open. Inside the sack were a bunch of rocks and a note. The note said:

Welcome to Peru.
–Mateo and Julia.

Tony reaches into the mouth of the statue.

On the car ride home, Mateo and Julia told Tony all about the statue of Chavin, which was real. They told him about the snakes, which were harmless. And they told him how Mateo had been carrying the sack with him the whole time and stuck it in the statue when he ran ahead.

"Why?" asked Tony.

"We wanted you to have an adventure," said Mateo.

"And just maybe we wanted to teach our big-shot cousin a little lesson," added Julia.

"A lesson?" said Tony.

"Admit it, Tony," said Mateo. "You were pretty scared."

"Me? Scared? Never." said Tony.

Mateo rolled his eyes at Julia. It didn't matter what Tony said. He had been **terrified.** They had gotten him good.

"So—what did you kids do today?" Uncle Marco asked over dinner that night.

"Just hung around," said Tony, winking at Mateo.

"I'm sorry if you're not having fun here, Antonio," said Uncle Marco. "Oh—I mean Tony," he added.

Tony shrugged. "I think I'll be Antonio for the summer."

Uncle Marco looked pleased.

"Well, that's just fine," he said. "Now—what should we do this weekend?"

Tony smiled. "Oh, we'll think of something," he said. He was going to think of something, all right. He had all summer to plan his revenge.

Glossary

attitude *(noun)* opinions and feelings about someone or something (p. 9)

canopy *(noun)* a shelter over something (p. 31)

clutch *(verb)* to hold onto something tightly (p. 18)

culture *(noun)* the culture of a group of people is their way of life, ideas, customs, and traditions (p. 16)

counselor *(noun)* a person who works at a summer camp with children (p. 6)

glare *(verb)* to look at someone in a very angry way (p. 14)

grumble *(verb)* to complain about something in a grouchy way (p. 7)

legend *(noun)* a story handed down from earlier times (p. 14)

panic *(noun)* a sudden feeling of terror (p. 23)

plead *(verb)* to beg (p. 13)

preserve *(noun)* a place where animals and plants are protected (p. 17)

shuffle *(verb)* to walk slowly, hardly moving your feet (p. 13)

terrified *(adverb)* to be greatly frightened (p. 34)

vampire bat *(noun)* a bat in South America that feeds on the blood of birds and other animals (p. 28)